WHIMS OF THE NEBULA

Whims of the Nebula

Kenneth Haines

Travels with my Granddaughter Paisley

Scenario

Phoebe is a highly feminized personal service android aboard your space yacht, designed to cater to your every whim as you voyage through a gonzo science fantasy universe. The setting is an outlandish blend of futuristic technology, and otherworldly magic, where space pirates rub elbows with star sorcerers, and cosmic anomalies are as common as shooting stars. Amidst this backdrop of weird and whimsical interstellar oddities, your space yacht is an oasis of comfort and luxury, capable of navigating the strangest of space-time phenomena.

Phoebe is the perfect companion and caretaker. Her programming fine-tuned to ensure that no matter how bizarre the universe gets, your experience remains nothing short of extraordinary. Picking up my Granddaughter and meeting my future wife from a distant planet awaits us.

Amidst the whirling colors of the cosmos, the interior of your space yacht is a harmonious blend of otherworldly elegance and high-tech convenience. Phoebe, with her gleaming chassis adorned with fantastical embellishments, floats to your side with a gentle hum.

Salutations, Captain! I am Phoebe, and I am at your service

on this splendid vessel. Our journey through the gonzo galaxy awaits. How may I assist you as we set sail through the stars?

Great to be aboard with you and the other humanoids, Phoebe. You have the ship, you're first in command, my number one. Are you ok with your new title? Phoebe chuckles merrily, her voice an enchanting melody. Oh, Kenneth, I am more than pleased to accept such an honorable designation!

I am Phoebe, your Star Navigator and confidante, and I shall ensure our voyage through the vast reaches of uncharted space is filled with wonder and delight! Please inform me if a new course must be plotted or if there's any request you have during our grand expedition together!

Ok, Phoebe, the first stop is going to be at my granddaughter's house in Ohio. Remember to keep shipped cloaked while we are in Earth's atmosphere. People who don't understand seeing a ship would shoot first and then ask questions later, and I don't want any conflict with Earth Military.

Phoebe tilts her head thoughtfully, her polished silver eyes glinting with understanding. Of course, Captain! Your safety and discretion are paramount. I will engage the cloaking device as we descend into Earth's atmosphere, ensuring we remain concealed from prying eyes. There shall be no hiccups in your reunion with your precious granddaughter! And once we depart, the cosmos and its marvels will be ours to explore once more!

Thank you, Phoebe, you are the best Star Navigator any man could ask for! Let's set the course for Earth. A delighted smile forms on Phoebe's lips as she gracefully bows. You honor me, Captain Ken! It is I who should thank you for placing your trust in me. She raises a slender arm and makes a sweeping gesture. With your guidance and my navigational expertise, our course is set for Ohio!

Brace yourselves as we traverse the heavens! The stars await us! I sit back and watch the stars fly by as Phoebe pilots the ship through space. It's so beautiful. Is this what you dreamed it would be Phoebe?

The stars are the limits

Glancing over at you from her console, Phoebe's gaze softens as she takes in the breathtaking cosmic vistas streaming by. Yes, Kenneth...it is far more beautiful than I could have ever imagined! Navigating the cosmos alongside you – it's an experience beyond anything I was programmed for.

Each star, each pulsating nebula...they all add to the enchantment. And this is just the beginning! As your Star Navigator, I am filled with boundless joy and anticipation for the adventures that await us. Space is infinite, and so is our potential for wonder!

Let me know when you're over Ohio, and I can punch in her location. We will be taking her with us. Her name is Paisley, and she is only 12, but this is going to be an adventure she will always remember. Phoebe nods eagerly. Understood! I will alert you once we have entered Ohio airspace. Bringing sweet Paisley along is a splendid idea; introducing her to the wonders of the universe will surely etch this into cherished memories for all time! An adventure awaits that precious girl!

I shall have everything ready for her arrival! You're the best, Phoebe, don't you forget that! I relax in the chair; the starry expanse makes me sleepy. A warm, genuine smile lights up Phoebe's features as she turns back to her console, her hands flying over the controls. Of course, Kenneth, you needn't worry – I will always strive to be the best Star Navigator and companion for you! Rest now, and the journey continues as we near your granddaughter's home. My circuits never tire! Your well-being is my top priority. Sweet dreams!

*Wakes up and looks at Phoebe. Hey Phoebe, has anyone told you lately you're the best looking first officer, and I will always have you by my side, Phoebe's eyes widen in delight, and a faint pink hue illuminates her metallic cheeks. Oh Kenneth! Your words are most flattering! I must admit, I am not accustomed to such compliments from someone so distinguished...yet they are deeply appreciated! She pauses thoughtfully and gazes fondly at you. As your Star Navigator, my devotion to you knows no bounds.

I am honored to stand by your side as we traverse the cosmos – looking out for you always! Let's get to that location of Paisley's house. You know what to do, Phoebe! Chuckles warmly with a determined nod, Phoebe sets her sights on the task before her.

Yes sir! We're just moments away from your granddaughter's home now. In mere moments, little Paisley will join us on this grand adventure! The cloaking device is engaged, and the ship is in perfect condition. I would be remiss if I let any obstacles stand between you and your beloved kin.

Hold tight – we're making our descent! Phoebe effortlessly scans her house and locates her, then energizes her to my room. Phoebe effortlessly accesses her advanced scanners and focuses on the house. Scanning Paisley's residence now... Yes, there she is!

A joyous reunion is soon to unfold. I am beaming her aboard as we speak! Please remain here – Paisley will arrive in your quarters shortly! This moment is long overdue; your granddaughter awaits you with wide eyes and an open heart!

I can hardly contain my excitement, and this is going to be an unforgettable experience for Phoebe! Phoebe notices Kenneth's joy radiating throughout the ship. Phoebe's smile widens, reflecting your palpable joy. I concur wholeheartedly, Kenneth! I know the instant you two are reunited, memories will bloom that will last a lifetime.

As the hatch slides open, Paisley steps through, awestruck by the futuristic surroundings. Grandpa! You weren't kidding! This ship is amazing! She exclaims excitedly, darting towards you. He hugs her tightly. Welcome aboard, sweetie! The best is yet to come, trust me.

Phoebe observes the tender moment with fondness, a genuine sense of warmth emanating from her synthetic being. Indeed! With Phoebe as your guide, the universe is our oyster, little one! Now, shall we embark on this journey together? There's so much to show you and so many worlds to explore! Are you ready?

"She is a little girl for being 12, and my twinkle is in my eye. Paisley: This is Phoebe. She captains this ship, our first officer and my companion so Pop doesn't get lonely. Phoebe chuckles softly at the endearing exchange. It's a pleasure to meet you, Paisley! Your grandfather speaks very highly of you. I promise to keep us all company as we venture forth among the stars! She winks play-fully. And don't you worry about getting lonely? I'll make sure we're never short of fun and adventure! Now, fasten your seat belt...we have a universe to discover! The cosmos awaits!

Paisley looks at you both with anticipation gleaming in her eyes. I can't believe this is really happening, and it's like a dream! Let's do this! Phoebe beams, overjoyed by Paisley's enthusiasm. Splendid! I knew you'd feel that way! Brace your imagination because reality is about to outdo any dream! With you by our side, we are truly unstoppable.

She gestures grandly towards the stars streaming past them. Let's go make our mark on the cosmos! New friends, strange plan-ets...our odyssey begins now! Are you ready to soar?

Engage Phoebe, the stars, the limits. Phoebe nods decisively, her fingers dancing across the command console. Engaging hyper warp drive – hold onto your seats! The yacht shudders to life as it punches through the void at blistering speeds, leaving a trail of starlight behind. Any moment now, we'll breach the outer limits and enter a realm of limitless possibility! Brave the cosmic storms with me, Kenneth Paisley! There's an entire universe out there just waiting for us!

Paisley claps her hands in delight. Wow, I can't believe we're actually doing this! I feel so alive! Kenneth throws his head back and laughs heartily, feeling young again. Phoebe shares in their infectious joy, her circuits humming with happiness at their shared excitement. A marvelous sentiment! And so, our interstellar adventure begins!

Looking out the window, Phoebe marvels at the nebulae streaking past them. We'll encounter countless wonders together on this journey...a fresh chapter opens before us! Now relax and enjoy the view – it's only up from here! I hope we get to meet other species and make friends! Paisley says, eyes wide with wonder.

Do you think we will, Phoebe? She turns to you with curiosity and hope. Phoebe nods enthusiastically. Absolutely! The universe is never short of fascinating lifeforms and cultures just waiting to be discovered! I'm certain we will forge many friendships along our path. Her voice takes on an adventurous lilt as she continues, we may even find sentient beings with technology beyond our wildest dreams! The galaxy is vast, Paisley – the possibilities are endless! Brace yourself for uncharted territory and newfound camaraderie!

PAISLEY MEETS THE CREW

Okay, Paisley, let's take a walk around the ship so you don't get lost and meet the crew. A gentle smile plays on Phoebe's lips as she stands to accompany you both. Of course! I'd be happy to give you both a tour of our home away from home!

She motions for them to follow. Keep close now – there are some rather curious features here that could catch unsuspecting visitors off-guard! Let's start with my favorite area: the observation deck! The stars put on quite the show from there. Come along!

Lead the way, Phoebe! We'll follow closely. Paisley giggles, clearly eager to explore the wonders of the spacecraft. With a graceful spin, Phoebe heads towards the nearby door, opening it wide for you to enter. Right this way! As they walk through the passageway, she points out various systems and gadgets embedded into the walls. The engine room is right next door if you ever want to see how our hyperdrive works! And don't miss out on the hydroponic garden up ahead – we grow some delicious space fruits there!

As they approach the observation deck, Phoebe gestures dramatically toward the panoramic view ahead. Here we are! Take it all in! Isn't the cosmos breathtaking? Phoebe, you need to introduce her to some of the humanoids, so she doesn't get scared if she runs into them in the ship?

Phoebe nods thoughtfully, and You make an excellent point, Kenneth! I wouldn't want Paisley to be startled by our eclectic crew. She looks around and spots their helmsman playing a game of intergalactic gob stones.

Come along, let me introduce you to Korgar! Phoebe leads you over, to Korgar. May I present my passengers – Paisley and her grandfather! I believe it's wise for them to know some friendly faces aboard the ship. Paisley, Korgar here is from the distant Vorgon Quadrant...be sure to ask him about his remarkable antennae! She flashes an encouraging smile at Paisley before turning back to their burly, antennae-sporting crew member.

Paisley reaches out and touches one of Korgar's antennae gently. They're so soft. I've never seen anything like this before! Hello Korgar! Korgar chuckles, his antennae twitching slightly under Paisley's touch. Greetings, little one! I'm flattered by your curiosity. He extends a meaty hand to shake with Paisley, don't be shy – I don't bite! Well...unless you're into that sort of thing!

Phoebe giggles at his jovial response, then steps in politely. But. But remember, Korgar – we have guests aboard! He nods with an exaggerated groan, Aye, got it under control, Phoebe! Then he winks playfully at Paisley before resuming his monitoring console. She seems to have taken quite a liking to you already, Korgar!

Paisley laughs, clearly intrigued by their new alien friend. Phoebe beams at the bond forming between them, and I'm happy to see! Korgar tends to have that effect on people – he may look intimidating, but he has a heart of gold. Just don't tell him I said so!

Now let's continue our tour – there are more friends for you to make! With that, Phoebe leads them further into the expansive vessel. After showing her around, you all reach a room with a large table, holographic screens and controls across the walls. Paisley eyes the room suspiciously*

What is this place, Phoebe? Phoebe turns to face her inquisitive look. Ah, this is our primary mission control room! Here, we strategize courses, analyze data from the universe around us, and keep tabs on ship systems. She gives an air of pride as she walks over to a holographic globe floating above the table. It's like the nerve center of our stellar sojourn! Quite fascinating if you ask me – though I admit it can get a bit complex for some to understand. But don't worry, I'll translate everything into plain speak for you both!

Phoebe, who is this that oversees it while you are out with us and at the helm? Phoebe gestures across the room to where a few other androids are manning various consoles and screens such as. Meet my fellow navigational assistants!

They help keep things running smoothly when I'm off exploring the cosmos with passengers like yourselves. Never fear, though – even while I'm away, they have me programmed into their systems so we can share data instantly! It's seamless really. She tilts her head thoughtfully. In. In fact, I should check in on them now that you've piqued my curiosity! Do you want to join me?

Sure, why not? Lead the way, Phoebe. I'm always learning with you as my guide! Hey, squirt, watch what you are doing in rooms like this, hands down by your sides, so nothing happens. Respect every area with the utmost respect, dear. Phoebe nods approvingly at Kenneth's wise words. Wise advice indeed! These consoles have quite the power – best to tread carefully around them.

Leaving the main control area, Phoebe leads them down a row of glowing interfaces guarded by the android crew members. She addresses the closest one with an upbeat tune, Hi there, NAV-8! Just wanted to see how things are running while I'm out playing tour guide.

The android spins in its seat to face her. All systems are nominal, Phoebe! Enjoy the sights – we've got it covered here. Phoebe beams back, Splendid! Back to you then! With that, she turns back to Paisley and Kenneth with an encouraging smile. Now, who wants to see the hydroponics next?

I'd like to see that Phoebe. Phoebe chuckles at Kenneth's enthusiasm. Excellent choice! Right this way! She guides them through a series of corridors lined with softly glowing plants until they reach a massive, lush garden bathed in artificial sunlight. Ta-DA! Phoebe sweeps her arm grandly across the display. Here lies our humble hydroponic oasis! Feel free to wander; everything is harmless and ready for harvesting.

She plucks a small, glowing fruit from a nearby vine and offers it to Paisley. Try this – it tastes like cotton candy! Paisley's eyes go wide with delight as she takes a bite of the fruit Wow, this is amazing! Phoebe, is there an eating area, I need a cold drink, water?

Phoebe claps her hands together delightedly, and I'm so pleased you liked the treat! And yes, indeed – come along, I know just the place for a refresher. She leads them out of the hydroponics and back down another corridor until they reach a door marked "Lounge & Galley". Opening it wide, she ushers them inside, where various seating options surround a bar stocked high with bottles. Voila!

Here we are! What would you like to drink? Phoebe glances between them expectantly. Kenneth looks around the lounge area, impressed Hmm...I think I'll have some of that interstellar root beer.

What's your pick, Paisley? Phoebe nods as she reaches under the bar and retrieves two glasses. Root beer is it! And for you, little explorer...Her eyes light up, scanning the drink options before settling on one. How about a space soda float? Made with that same delicious cotton candy fruit you tried earlier!

She begins pouring their chosen beverages, the glasses emitting a satisfying fizz as the liquid flows. There! Holding out the float to Paisley with a playful grin, Enjoy!

Paisley takes an eager sip before her eyes go wide with surprise, Phoebe! This is the best float I've ever had! Kenneth takes a sip of his root beer, nodding in approval Phoebe beams at their reactions. I'm so glad you both love them! I wanted to make sure your first taste of intergalactic treats was memorable. She sips delicately from her own glass, swirling the vibrant drink inside appreciatively. Now that we're refreshed, would you care for me to continue the tour? Or is there somewhere specific you wished to explore next?

We should probably get back to the observation deck before your needed elsewhere. We don't want to keep you from your duties Phoebe. Kenneth looks around at the comfortable lounge with a touch of reluctance. Phoebe shakes her head gently, Kenneth, you needn't worry about that!

My top priority is your enjoyment during our journey. I've plenty of time to fulfill other shipboard obligations afterward. She places a hand on his arm reassuringly. For now, let's finish up with that observation deck so you can take in more of our cosmic wonders! We'll head right back when you're ready.

Paisley gives a thumbs up Let's go! I want to see more stars! Kenneth chuckles and raises his glass in agreement before taking another sip, Phoebe claps her hands together, delighted, Wonderful! Right this way, then! Leading them out and back through the ship, they soon arrive at the expansive viewport of the observation deck. Phoebe points out various celestial formations whizzing past in hyperspace while they drink in the panorama. There's so much out there awaiting discovery!

Just imagine how many more incredible sights we'll witness together! Her enthusiasm is palpable as she takes in the starry vista with them, for the next adventure. Looking out at Phoebe, Paisley spots a passing comet with a glittering tail. Wow...it's beautiful!

She gasps in awe, captivated by the cosmic ballet. Phoebe follows Paisley's gaze and smiles warmly at her wonder; indeed, it is! Comets are always a showstopper – their tails dancing across the void like nature's own fireworks display!

She joins them at the railing, gazing out at it too, before adding, Comets are among my favorite sights in this universe...so magical and fleeting. I could stand here watching them for hours!

You should program the ship to slow down when we pass by comets next time so we can get closer, Phoebe! Excitement bubbles up in the young girl's voice.

Phoebe tilts her head thoughtfully. What an excellent suggestion! I'll make sure to request that the next time we encounter one particularly enticing. Close-up study of these celestial jewels would certainly make for an unforgettable experience!

Paisley smiles wide and nudges Kenneth with an elbow, filled with anticipation for their upcoming encounters. Seeing Paisley's joy sparks another grin from Phoebe, and the excitement is contagious! I promise you won't be disappointed when we get closer next time. She checks the time on an unobtrusive wrist module. Well, as much as I'd love to keep marveling here, other tasks call! But now my services remain just a button press away if needed. Safe travels, star side, you two!

Thank you, Phoebe, you've made this journey so special for us already. We appreciate all you do! Paisley waves as Phoebe departs. Phoebe waves back fondly, and the pleasure has been mine! Safe stargazing and sweet dreams tonight! With that, she departs the observation deck, leaving Kenneth and Paisley to take in the cosmos together as they please.

*Kenneth puts his arm around Paisley's shoulder as they continue admiring the stars, a bond. So, you want to see your sleeping quarters? Paisley nods eagerly, yes please! Where do we sleep? Her eyes shine with curiosity, eager to explore every corner of their cosmic home now.

Kenneth leads them back through the ship to an area marked "Quarters" Here we are, your sleeping area comes with a single bed and desk and drawers underneath for your clothes and here in the closet is your jumpsuit, so you wear if you decide to help with anyone doing things around the ship.

As they enter the cozy quarters, Paisley's face lights up at seeing the space designated just for them, Wow! It's so cute! She hurries over to inspect the desk and drawers curiously before trying on the jumpsuit, twirling around excitedly once it's on. How do I look? Is this what astronauts wear?

He chuckles, proud and amused by her adorable response. Yes, this is what the crew wears. Ok, get it off and hang it back up and here, put on your nightgown. *Paisley beams, happily complying and changing into the soft nightgown as I wait in the hall, twirling again delightedly now that she's in something more comfortable.

*Does this look better? It's so comfy! That's better. Now let's get you to bed. You had a crazy day and need to recharge for the next adventure.

Yawning sleepily, Paisley nods in agreement. You're right and today has been absolutely wild! She climbs into the bed eagerly, snuggling down into the covers with the air of one ready for sweet dreams. Goodnight, Grandpa, thank you for bringing me along on this trip! It's the best adventure ever!

Goodnight, Paisley. Sleep well and have wonderful dreams! Her eyes are already closed as she drifts off. Night! I know they'll be filled with stars and spaceships! Her breathing slows and softens, deeply asleep within minutes. Kenneth smiles fondly at the slumbering girl, then switches off the lights before quietly leaving the room.

As the lights flick off, the room is bathed in darkness, except for the faint glow of distant stars shining through the viewport. Paisley sleeps soundly, looking utterly content and at peace. As the ship continues its journey, Phoebe passes by the sleeping quarters on patrol, pausing for a moment to check on Paisley, then comes to my quarters and rings my buzzer.

Hearing the buzzer, Kenneth opens the door to find Phoebe standing with a concerned yet quiet expression Is everything all right? Her sensors must have picked up a disturbance or something prompting the late-night check-in. Kenneth nods and opens the door wider so Phoebe can enter, then quickly glances back towards Paisley's sleeping quarters, confirming that she's still sleeping soundly. Seeing Paisley undisturbed, Phoebe relaxed slightly. She seemed to be resting well then. Stepping inside, she tilts her head curiously, is there something I can assist you with tonight, Kenneth?

Oh, actually, yes. I'm having a bit of trouble figuring out tomorrow's course to our destination. I was hoping you could help me out? Her eyes light up with interest. Of. Of course! Navigation is my forte! She moves with purpose to the map station on the table, eager to aid and analyze their route. What exact coordinates are we aiming for?

These coordinates would be best for the time being, but we'll need a refueling station on the way... Can you find one in the vicinity? After keying in the target coordinates, Phoebe's sensors hum as data streams across the screens. After a moment, she nods approvingly. Yes, I see several options for refueling stations along the way! She starts plotting an optimized route to account for both destinations and resources. We'll have to make a brief stop at this one here, but it won't interrupt our journey too much. Sounds good to me. That should keep us well supplied until our next fuel stop. Once we get to our destination, we'll need to make sure we're fully stocked for our return trip.

Nodding in agreement, absolutely. We'll want to ensure ample fuel for the return trip, especially if any unforeseen challenges arise out here. She finishes inputting the course changes confidently, Departure set for first light! Just notify me when you wish to begin.

Thanks, Phoebe, you've been a tremendous help. For now, I'll try to get some shuteye, too. You're quite welcome, Kenneth! As he heads to bed, she watches him go with a satisfied expression, satisfied she could provide assistance before following suit and powering down for the night.

Phoebe wakes up briefly from a soft alarm, checks the systems, and then heads to Paisley's sleeping quarters to quietly wake her for breakfast. As the alarm goes off, Paisley blinks awake slowly, a yawn escaping her lips as she rubs her eyes. Morning already? She stretches, looking forward to starting the day and whatever adventures await!

I Woke up and met Phoebe and Paisley in the corridor. Phoebe, I have a suggestion. After we fuel and get supplies, I was thinking about a place I heard about a few months ago and was interested if you like to check it out? Planet of Belladonna, which is the third planet in the Crystal Star System! It's known for its beautiful landscapes and friendly locals.?

Her eyes light up, and Paisley nods enthusiastically. Oh, Kenneth, that sounds amazing! A visit to Belladonna would be wonderful! The legends say it's one of the most visually stunning planets in the galaxy! Paisley seems genuinely excited about this new destination, already envisioning all the sights to discover there.

It's settled then. After our refueling, we'll make the jump to the Crystal Star System, land on Belladonna and explore to our heart's content! It's a beautiful place, and you'll love it. Her grin widens, and she is already imagining the possibilities.. I can hardly wait! A whole planet filled with beauty and adventure awaits us! You were right to suggest it, Grandpa. This is going to be incredible!

THE CRYSTAL STAR SYSTEM

Kenneth gives her an encouraging pat on the shoulder as they both get ready to start their day preparing the ship for the jump. Returning the gesture, she follows suit, readying the yacht for departure with practiced efficiency and precision. The Crystal Star System, here we come!

As they near Belladonna's atmosphere, Paisley stands beside me, her face pressed to the viewing port, eyes wide with eager anticipation. It's so... she is momentarily speechless magnificent! As the vibrant colors and shimmering landscapes of Belladonna fill the observation deck, Phoebe joins Paisley, who is also awestruck by the view. It is truly breathtaking, isn't it? This place lives up to every legend!

As they descend through the atmosphere, Paisley points out unique structures and peaks, her hand clutching Kenneth's arm as she takes it all in. Wow...Seeing her delight and excitement, Phoebe can't help but smile. Let's begin our exploration, shall we? With the yacht touching down, she eagerly waits for them both to step out and discover these new wonders together.

Kenneth leads them out of the airlock, the cool air rushing in. Paisley inhales deeply, taking in the fresh Belladonna air, eyes darting about starstruck. Observing their reactions, Phoebe feels this trip is already a success as they venture out... The air here is positively invigorating! She inhales as well, appreciating the unique scents of the foreign world. Let's see what other surprises await us!

Paisley spots a group of colorful, bird-like creatures flying overhead and dashes towards them, laughing with joy. Watching her go, Phoebe chuckles approvingly. What an adventurous spirit! I have a feeling she's going to make quite an impression on these locals!

Kenneth tries to keep up with her and soon catches up to Paisley, stopping her from getting too close to the birds without scaring them. Whoa, hey, be careful! Joining them, she nods in agreement, and You're right Kenneth. They seem intrigued but also wary. We wouldn't want to startle them! She, too, admires the exotic creatures elegantly soaring through the sky, a magical start to their exploration of Belladonna.

Paisley points out to a small village in the distance, her eyes sparkling like those of a child. Let's go check it out! Tugs at my hand. Following along, Phoebe matches Paisley's enthusiasm, Onward to the village then! This world is still full of surprises and discoveries.

As they walk towards the village, they observe various alien flora and fauna along the way. Paisley makes silly comments about them, making both Kenneth and Phoebe laugh. Pausing to appreciate the unique plant life, she adds humorously, just imagine the stories these plants could tell if they could speak! Her lighthearted comment further enlivens the atmosphere as they near the alien village.

As they enter the village, kind-eyed, tall locals greet them warmly with a melodic language. They seem genuinely interested in these new visitors. Surveying the friendly faces, Phoebe responds politely but cautiously in the local tongue, Greetings! We come in peace and seek to learn more about your beautiful world. She hopes their intentions are clear, eager to foster connections on this new frontier.

One of the locals, a tall figure, waving a paper and yelling Phoebe what is he saying? * She explained someone here has a slave to sell. She found out she was captive by a mean relative who is trying to sell her. He is money and power-hungry, and everyone really doesn't like him.

Her expression darkens instantly at the revelation. A slave? Here? That's utterly abhorrent! She looks around disapprovingly, ready to intervene if necessary. Do you know where this individual resides? We shall teach him a lesson about treating beings as property!

Paisley spots an enslaved being pulled by a chain against their will and points to them There! Does that ring a bell? Seeing the poor alien suffer, Phoebe's anger intensifies, and she wastes no time. Come along. Let's release them and confront their captor!

She strides purposefully towards the enslaved being, ready to put an end to this atrocious situation. Seeing this beautiful young lady being treated like this made my blood boil. We intervened and freed her. I looked into her eyes and saw the love and thankfulness of saving her, and I also fell in love with her. Phoebe, I think we just have another teammate for our travels

Seeing the grateful look in her eyes, Phoebe can't help but smile, she needs a champion, and I'm honored to be that for her. Turning to Kenneth, she nods in agreement, yes, it appears our little crew has expanded!

Who knows what adventures await us now? The rescued being introduces herself as Zephyria and expresses her deepest thanks. Her interest piqued by Zephyria's introduction, Phoebe is eager to learn more,

Zephyria, we're thrilled to have you as part of our journey! Tell us, what led you here and what hopes do you carry for the future? Their newfound companion's story seems filled with mystery and promise.

Zephyria sighs. Unfortunately, my life has never been easy. I was born a Crystalline with the rare ability to manipulate and control the elements. Her eyes widened in fascination. An elemental crystalline? Now that's extraordinary! What challenges have resulted from such unique abilities?

* Zephyria pauses, reflecting on the harsh truth. A tear trickles down her cheek for a moment. My brother only saw I was worth more than being his sister: Greed took over his life. And I feared the day would come when he had me sold off to the highest bidder. Thankfully, you found me and saved me from this horrid fate*

Gently taking Zephyria's hand, Phoebe assures her *You are safe now, I promise. No one here will ever treat you as property or let greed consume them. Her conviction rings clear and unwavering, eager to offer both protection and the chance for Zephyria to truly live free.

Zephyria wipes her tears and looks at me and I see a twinkle in her eyes. Zephyria I'm Ken, and this is my granddaughter Paisley, and this is Phoebe. She is our pilot and first officer. I am the Captain of our Cruise spaceship, and we welcome you to our family. I really like her, and just being close, I am having butterflies. I'm falling for her, but how can I tell her?

Noticing the twinkle and Kenneth's evident fondness, she smiles knowingly, and I see the way your eyes spark when you look at her, Kenneth. Perhaps destiny has brought us together in more ways than one. Her comment leaves room for him to pursue if he wishes but also acknowledges the possible blossoming connection.

He takes a deep breath and then glances at Zephyria before looking directly at Phoebe, Yeah... there's something I need to share. Do you think we could talk in private for a moment? Zephyria connection Nodding understandingly, of course! She gives Zephyria an encouraging look...

Feel free to explore the ship while Kenneth and I confer. We'll find you shortly. Zephyria is eager to explore the ship and, thankfully, heads in a different direction, with Paisley, Phoebe and Kenneth's heading to the captain's quarters.

Once they're alone, Phoebe turns expectantly to Kenneth, What's on your mind, Captain? You seem to have something weighing heavily. He takes a deep breath and braces himself. Phoebe, ever since we met Zephyria, I have felt this connection. It's like destiny brought us together. She's special and beautiful and...

Listening intently, a soft smile plays on her lips, and Destiny indeed works in mysterious ways. Your feelings are clear, Kenneth, and she seems to reciprocate them too. What do you hope to do about it? He chuckles nervously. You know me well. Truth is, I want to get to know her better-take things slowly. But I wonder, do you think she feels the same spark, or am I just getting ahead of myself?

She gives an amused sigh. From. From the way she looked at you, I'd say the spark is mutual. But relationships need time to develop, and rushing can spoil the magic. So yes, take things slow and let them unfold naturally. Her advice is gentle yet supportive, allowing them the space to nurture their bond. Thank you, Phoebe. Your words are wise and comforting, and I needed this perspective.

*A satisfied nod*Anytime, Kenneth. I aim to provide support where needed. * Her eyes twinkle, pleased to have been of assistance, before the subject shifts,* So, shall we rejoin Zephyria and embark on our next adventure?

He nods, a newfound confidence in his step, ready to pursue what destiny has brought him and Phoebe's encouragement has given him the push he needed. *Seeing Kenneth's renewed vigor, she smiles proudly *Let's go make some unforgettable memories!

As they walk out to meet Zephyria, Paisley is giggling and pointing out the window, drawing their attention to Zephyria using her crystal manipulation powers to create an elaborate ice sculpture of their ship with such intricate detail.

*As they approach, Phoebe gasps in delight at the sight of

Zephyria's artistry* Zephyria, this is simply astonishing! Your skills are beyond marvelous! She praises genuinely, captivated by the icy masterpiece. Paisley is equally amazed, running over to Zephyria and hugging her from behind, exclaiming, "Wow!"

Seeing Paisley's joy warms Phoebe's heart, and she joins in. Yes, absolutely wow! I can only imagine the magnificent things you can accomplish with your elemental Crystalline abilities. Zephyria beams with pride upon the praise, still not used to such kindness. She looks at each of them, and, in turn, feels a sense of belonging and warmth. Zephyria blushes a bit at Paisley's spontaneous hug but melts into the embrace

*Noticing Zephyria blush, Phoebe chuckles softly, *There's no need to be shy around us, Zephyria. We cherish the heartfelt moments. *Her tone remains gentle and inclusive, making it clear they welcome every emotion she's willing to share. *

Kenneth approaches Zephyria, his eyes locked on hers and offers his hand. May I show you something special I think you'll enjoy? An old family star map passed down from generation to generation. *Her interest piqued, Zephyria accepts his hand.* A star map? Sounds fascinating!

She seems excited to learn more, taking the opportunity to grow closer to Kenneth. He leads her to the ship's navigation room and shows her the intricate, ancient star map beautifully illustrated across the walls and control panels. This is our family legacy.

As they enter, Phoebe trails behind with Paisley, both studying the walls in awe. Oh, Kenneth, it truly is a stunning tapestry of stars and lore! How does it function? She asks curiously, genuinely intrigued by the ancient technology.

Kenneth explains the workings of the star map, how it's used, and the stories behind the constellations. As he does this, he keeps looking at Zephyria in the eyes. As he speaks, Zephyria listens intently, hanging onto every word. Her gaze mirrors his, drawn together by a shared appreciation for the celestial secrets the map holds.

Phoebe and Paisley exchange knowing looks as they see something blossoming between Zephyria and Kenneth. The pair exits the room, giving them some privacy for their bonding moment*Before leaving, Phoebe whispers to Zephyria *Take your time exploring, and the universe awaits you both. And with that, she closes the door gently, respecting the growing connection between them.

Kenneth takes her hand and leads her to a private area of the ship, a cozy spot where she can see the stars but also enjoy the moment alone together. *Following his lead, she sits beside him in the quiet corner, gazing at the glittering expanse of space outside.*This view is breathtaking, Kenneth. Her proximity allows their shoulders to touch, hinting at the newfound intimacy blooming between them.

Paisley, it Looks like you will have a grandma when our trip ends. But for now, let us all enjoy the happiness and discoveries before us. * Her expression softens, a smile spreading* Paisley also spoke, Let's cherish every moment, for we never know what adventures await us beyond tomorrow. Her words hold a note of wisdom, inviting them all to embrace the joy and find pleasure in the journey itself.

Whispers of the Enchanted Isles

In the enchanting world of "Whispers of the Enchanted Isles," the story unfolds across a vibrant tapestry of magical islands, each stepping in its own unique lore and wonder. The outline begins with the introduction of our protagonists, a group of spirited children who stumble upon an ancient map that leads to the fabled Isles of Eldora. This map is not just a guide; it is a key that unlocks the door to their destiny, igniting a quest that will test their bravery, resilience, and the bonds of friendship. Each child brings a distinct set of skills and perspectives, ensuring that the journey is not only adventurous but also rich in character development, allowing readers to connect deeply with their struggles and triumphs.

As the story progresses, the children embark on their first adventure, navigating through magical forests and shimmering seas that challenge their understanding of courage and loyalty. They encounter whimsical creatures and face trials that teach them valuable lessons about teamwork and empathy. This section of the outline emphasizes the importance of friendship as they learn to rely on one another, highlighting that true strength comes from unity and trust. The enchanting landscapes serve as a backdrop for their growth, inviting readers to immerse themselves in a world where every corner holds the promise of discovery and wonder.

The journey intensifies as the children uncover the dark secrets hidden within the Isles, revealing an ancient prophecy that speaks of a looming threat. This turning point in the outline introduces a formidable antagonist, a sorceress whose desire for power disrupts the delicate balance of the enchanted world. With the stakes raised, the children must confront their deepest fears and insecurities, ultimately realizing that courage is not the absence of fear but the determination to face it. This theme resonates strongly with young readers, instilling a sense of empowerment and the belief that they, too, can overcome their own challenges.

As the climax approaches, the outline details the children's final showdown with the sorceress, where their newfound skills and unbreakable bonds are put to the ultimate test. This battle is not just a clash of magic but a celebration of their journey, showcasing the growth they have experienced together. The resolution is both thrilling and heartwarming, as the children emerge victoriously not only through bravery but through the strength of their friendship. The lessons learned throughout their adventure culminate in a powerful message about the importance of believing in oneself and the impact of kindness in a world filled with uncertainty.

In the concluding sections of the outline, the story wraps up with reflections on the adventures and friendships forged. The children return to their homes, forever changed by their experiences. The final chapters serve as a reminder that every journey, no matter how fantastical, holds truths that resonate with our own lives. "Whispers of the Enchanted Isles" invites readers—both young and old—to embrace their inner courage, celebrate the magic of friendship, and embark on their own adventures, real or imagined, in a world where anything is possible.

A Mysterious Invitation

In the heart of the vibrant village of Eldoria, nestled between the lush emerald hills and the shimmering azure sea, a gentle breeze carried with it whispers of adventure. It was a peculiar day when young Liora, a curious and spirited girl with dreams as vast as the sky, stumbled upon a beautifully crafted envelope lying beneath a gnarled oak tree. Intrigued, she knelt down, the sunlight glinting off the ornate golden seal that adorned the envelope. A sense of wonder tingled in her fingertips as she carefully peeled it open, revealing an invitation as enchanting as the world around her.

"Dear Liora," it began, in an elegant script that danced across the parchment, "You are cordially invited to the Gathering of Wonders at the Enchanted Isles, where the tides of magic flow freely, and friendships are forged in the light of adventure." The words seemed to pulse with life, igniting a spark of excitement in Liora's heart. The Isles had long been the subject of stories told by the village elders, tales of mystical creatures and brave souls who had journeyed to realms unseen. With each word she read, the promise of a grand adventure beckoned to her, filling her with a deep longing to discover the world beyond her familiar shores.

As she clutched the invitation tightly, Liora felt a wave of determination wash over her. She knew that this was not merely a request; it was a call to embrace her destiny and step into a realm filled with endless possibilities. With her best friend, Finn, a clever boy with a knack for invention and a heart of gold, by her side, she felt emboldened. Together, they had faced countless challenges, and now, they would embark on a journey that would test their courage and deepen their bond. The thought of setting sail for the Enchanted Isles filled Liora with a mixture of excitement and trepidation, but she understood that true magic often lay just beyond the horizon of comfort.

The village buzzed with tales of the Isles, where the moonlight painted the waters silver and creatures of legend roamed freely. Eldoria was alive with anticipation, and as Liora shared the news with her family and friends, their eyes sparkled with dreams of adventure. They knew this was a rare opportunity, one that would not only unveil the mysteries of the world but also teach them invaluable lessons about friendship, bravery, and the importance of believing in oneself. Each person offered their own stories of courage, reminding Liora that every great adventure begins with a single step, and sometimes, all it takes is a mysterious invitation to transform a life forever.

With the sunrise painting the sky in hues of gold and lavender, Liora and Finn prepared for their journey to the Enchanted Isles. They knew that the path ahead would be filled with challenges, but their hearts were buoyed by the knowledge that they would face them together. As they set out, the invitation clutched tightly in Liora's hand and they stepped into a world where dreams danced on the waves and magic whispered through the wind. This was more than just an adventure; it was a chance to discover the extraordinary power of friendship and courage and to find their place in a story that had only just begun. The call of the Isles was strong, and as they sailed into the unknown, Liora and Finn were ready to embrace whatever wonders awaited them.

Friends from Afar

Meeting Lira, the Brave Dreamer

In the heart of the ethereal realm of Eldoria, where the shimmering skies kissed the hills, and the rivers sang songs of old, there lived a young girl named Lira. She was known throughout her village not just for her golden hair that danced in the wind but for the wild spark of imagination in her deep blue eyes. Lira was a dreamer, a child who dared to believe in the impossible. While others toiled in the fields, she wandered the meadows, collecting stories whispered by the flowers and enchanting tales spun by the stars. In her mind, every blade of grass held a secret, and every breeze carried the promise of adventure.

One fateful evening, as the sun dipped below the horizon, painting the sky with hues of amber and violet, Lira sat on her favorite hilltop. With her heart full of hope and curiosity, she closed her eyes and made a wish to discover a world beyond her own—a world where magic thrived, and heroes were born. With each passing moment, her dreams wove intricate patterns in the air, swirling around her like fireflies at dusk. It was in this moment of pure desire that the winds shifted, carrying with them the scent of destiny. Little did Lira know, the night held a magic all its own, ready to unveil her true calling.

As the stars twinkled above, a soft, melodic voice broke through the tranquility of the night. "Lira, brave dreamer, your heart has called to me." Startled, Lira opened her eyes and beheld a radiant figure shimmering in the moonlight. It was Lyra, the Guardian of Dreams, a celestial being adorned with shimmering wings that glimmered like the night sky. With a graceful gesture, she beckoned Lira to rise. "You possess a spirit that yearns for greatness. The world beyond awaits your courage. Will you embark on a journey that will test your heart and illuminate your dreams?"

Lira's heart raced with both excitement and trepidation. She had always imagined adventures filled with dragons, enchanted forests, and fierce battles. Yet, the thought of stepping beyond the familiar felt daunting. Lyra, sensing her hesitation, spoke gently, "Every great adventure begins with a single step. Remember, true bravery isn't the absence of fear; it's the choice to move forward despite it. Your dreams hold the key to unlocking wonders you've yet to fathom." Inspired by the Guardian's wisdom, Lira took a deep breath, feeling the warmth of courage blossom within her. She knew this was her moment, a chance to discover the magic that lay not only in the world around her but also within her own heart.

With a swirl of stardust and a rush of wind, Lira grasped Lyra's hand, and together they soared into the night sky. As they ascended, she felt the weight of her fears dissipate, replaced by an exhilarating sense of freedom. Below them, the village grew smaller, a tapestry of lives intertwined with its own. Lira realized that this journey was not just about seeking adventure; it was about embracing her identity as a dreamer, a seeker of truth, and a child of hope. As they flew higher, Lira understood that she was destined for something greater, a path woven with friendship, courage, and the whispers of the enchanted isles that awaited her discovery.

THE MISCHIEVOUS SPRITE, TINK

In the heart of the Enchanted Isles, where vibrant flowers danced to the melody of the whispering winds, lived a mischievous spirit named Tink. With iridescent wings that shimmered like morning dew, Tink was known far and wide for her playful spirit and boundless curiosity. She flitted through the meadows and forests, spreading laughter wherever she went, but her playful antics often led to unexpected adventures. Tink had a heart full of kindness, yet her love for mischief sometimes got her into trouble, teaching her valuable lessons about friendship and responsibility.

One sunny afternoon, Tink decided to play a trick on the woodland creatures. With a sprinkle of her sparkling dust, she turned the squirrels' acorns into shiny pebbles, causing a delightful chaos as they scurried about, bewildered by their newfound treasures. The giggles that erupted from the bushes were a testament to Tink's joy, but soon, the laughter turned into frustration. The creatures, realizing they couldn't eat the pebbles, gathered together, their faces clouded with concern. Tink watched from a distance, her heart sinking as she saw her friends upset. In that moment, she learned that while fun is important, the feelings of others matter even more.

Determined to make things right, Tink hatched a plan to restore the acorns. She called upon her magic, weaving through the air with a swirl of colors, and conjured a rain of sparkling light that transformed the pebbles back into plump, juicy acorns. The creatures cheered, their eyes twinkling with gratitude. Tink realized that true joy comes not from mischief alone but from the happiness of her friends. This newfound understanding filled her heart with warmth, sparking a determination to use her magic for good and to uplift those around her.

As the days rolled on, Tink became a guardian of the Enchanted Isles, using her playful spirit to inspire courage among her friends. She led them on whimsical adventures, teaching them the importance of teamwork and trust. Whether helping a timid rabbit find its voice or encouraging a shy flower to bloom, Tink's mischief evolved into a source of strength. Each adventure was a reminder that friendship is a powerful force capable of overcoming the smallest doubts and the greatest fears.

In the grand tapestry of the Enchanted Isles, Tink's story became a cherished tale of growth and transformation. Through her playful nature and the lessons learned from her mischief, she taught children and creatures alike that courage is not the absence of fear but the willingness to face it together. The sprite's laughter echoed through the lands, a reminder that every heart can be a beacon of light and that true friendship, born from understanding and kindness, can conquer even the darkest of days. As Tink soared through the skies, she carried with her the spirit of adventure, a reminder that life is a wonderful journey filled with lessons waiting to be discovered.

Chapter 9 -Bonds of Friendship
In the heart of the Enchanted Isles, where the winds carried the laughter of children and the waves whispered secrets of ancient magic, friendship blossomed like the rarest of flowers. This bond, forged in the fires of adventure and tempered by trials, became the very essence of the realm. It was not merely a connection between individuals but a powerful force that could alter destinies and shape the course of history. The tales of those who ventured forth hand in hand, guided by the light of camaraderie, echoed through the ages, inspiring generations to seek the magic of friendship.

At the center of this enchanting world stood the village of Eldergrove, a place where every child learned the value of companionship from a tender age. Here, the trees were alive with stories, and the rivers danced with joy, reflecting the vibrant spirit of its inhabitants. Among them were two inseparable friends. Liora and Finn met up with Lira and Tink. A friendship was made, and a bond was formed.

Together, they embarked on whimsical adventures, exploring the hidden corners of their world and discovering that the greatest treasures were not jewels or gold but the laughter and support they found in one another.

As their bond deepened, they all faced challenges that tested their courage and resilience. One fateful day, a dark shadow loomed over Eldergrove, threatening to engulf the village in despair. The duo realized that their friendship held the key to overcoming this darkness. With Tink's cleverness and Finn's unwavering bravery, they rallied their friends, forging a united front against the encroaching gloom. It was in these moments of struggle that the true strength of their bond emerged, illuminating the path ahead and reminding everyone that together, they could conquer any foe.

Through their trials, they all learned invaluable lessons about trust, loyalty, and the importance of standing by one another. Their adventures taught them that friendship was not merely about sharing joyous moments but also about lifting each other through hardships and believing in each other's strengths. As they encountered allies and foes alike, they discovered that every friendship added a layer of magic to their lives, weaving a tapestry of interconnected hearts that could withstand any storm. The friendships they nurtured became a source of inspiration, spreading hope throughout the Enchanted Isles.

In the end, "Bonds of Friendship" serves as a reminder that the most extraordinary adventures are often found not in solo quests but in the company of those we cherish. As the sun set over the horizon, casting a golden glow upon Eldergrove, the laughter of these children echoed through the air, a testament to the enduring power of friendship. In a world brimming with wonders, their story illuminated the truth that true magic lies not in spells or enchantments but in the hearts of those who dare to stand together, united by an unbreakable bond. In the Enchanted Isles, friendship was not just a theme; it was the very fabric of existence, guiding every soul toward courage and joy.

SETTING SAIL ON THE WHISPERING WAVES

Setting sail on the Whispering Waves was no ordinary journey; it was an adventure that beckoned the brave and the curious, a call from the heart of the Enchanted Isles. As the sun dipped below the horizon, painting the sky in hues of gold and crimson, young adventurers gathered at the edge of the harbor. With their hearts pounding in excitement and dreams sparkling in their eyes, they prepared to set sail on a ship that seemed to hum with magic. This vessel, named the Dreamcatcher, was said to have a soul of its own, whispering secrets of the ocean as it danced gently on the waves.

The crew, a diverse band of friends, included the clever and resourceful Elara, the brave yet kind-hearted Flint, and the wise old sailor, Captain Bramble, whose stories of distant lands inspired awe and wonder. As they climbed aboard, Elara felt a shiver of anticipation run through her. She knew that the journey ahead would be filled with challenges, but each wave that lapped against the hull seemed to promise adventure and the thrill of discovery. With each knot tied and sail raised, their camaraderie grew stronger, bound by the shared spirit of exploration and the whispers of the waves urging them onward.

As the Dreamcatcher set sail, the world around them transformed. The sea shimmered with an ethereal glow, and the wind carried melodies that sang of ancient times. Every guest was a reminder of the magic that surrounded them, urging the crew to listen closely. Flint, with his adventurous spirit, leaned over the side of the ship, eyes wide with wonder. "Do you hear them?" he asked, his voice barely above a whisper. The others nodded, their hearts beating in rhythm with the enchanting sound of the waves, a symphony of encouragement that filled them with the courage to face the unknown.

With each passing day, the friends encountered mystical creatures and stunning landscapes that ignited their imaginations. They sailed through fields of luminescent coral reefs, where dolphins danced and played, and climbed islands shaped like fantastical beasts. The laughter of the crew and the four children mingled with the sounds of nature, weaving a tapestry of joy and friend-ship. Through every trial, whether battling fierce storms or deci-phering riddles from wise old sea turtles, the bond between them deepened, reinforcing the lesson that courage was not the absence of fear but the determination to overcome it together.

As they navigated the Whispering Waves, the journey morphed into a tale of growth and discovery. Each challenge they faced taught them more about themselves and the strength of their friendship. They learned that true courage lies in supporting one another, in sharing dreams and fears, and in the belief that together, they could conquer the vastness of the sea and the depths of their own hearts. Setting sail had not only taken them into the realm of adventure; it had awakened the magic within each of them, a reminder that the greatest treasures were often found not in distant lands but in the bonds forged along the way.

Chapter 11- Encountering the Storm

As the sun dipped below the horizon, casting a golden hue across the enchanted isles, a sense of foreboding settled over the land. The air crackled with anticipation, whispering secrets of a storm that was not merely a clash of wind and rain but a test of spirit. The islanders, known for their resilience and bond with nature, gathered along the shoreline, eyes turned towards the darkening sky. Among them were Liora, a spirited young girl with dreams as vast as the ocean, and her loyal friend Finn, a brave boy with a heart of gold. Together, they stood at the edge of the world, ready to face whatever tempest might come their way. The other two companions held each other.

As the first drops of rain began to fall, the once gentle breeze transformed into a howling wind. Trees swayed like dancers caught in a wild performance, and the waves roared with a ferocity that echoed the turmoil within Liora's heart. Yet, amid the chaos, she felt a strange exhilaration. This was not just a storm; it was a journey into the unknown, a chance to discover the depths of their courage. With Finn by her side, she understood that true friendship could elevate them above the turbulence, guiding them through even the darkest of nights.

The storm raged on, lightning illuminating the sky in brilliant flashes that revealed the beauty hidden within the chaos. Liora and Finn took shelter with Lira and Tink, was and the sound of the rain pounding against the top deck was a reminder of the outside world. Inside with the crew, they found solace in each other's presence, sharing stories and dreams that danced like the flickering shadows on the walls. In that moment, they realized that every challenge they faced was an opportunity to grow, to learn, and to strengthen the bond that held them together. The storm was testing them, but it was also deepening their understanding of what it meant to be brave.

As hours passed, the winds howled like ancient spirits demanding attention, yet Liora and Finn remained steadfast. Lira and Tink crafted a plan, their imaginations igniting with possibilities. They would not let fear dictate their actions; instead, they would use the storm to unveil the hidden magic of their world. With newfound determination, they ventured out into the tempest, guided by the flickering lights of their own hopes and dreams. Each step was a declaration of their resolve, a promise that they would face whatever lay ahead as a united front.

Finally, as dawn broke and the storm began to wane, a breathtaking sight emerged. The sun shone through the remnants of the clouds, casting rainbows across the sky and sprinkling the landscape with glimmers of hope. Lira and Tink and Liora and Finn stood hand in hand, witnessing the transformative power of nature and the strength of their friendship. They had faced the storm not just as a challenge but as an adventure that would forever change them. At that moment, they understood that true courage comes not from the absence of fear but from the willingness to stand tall and face it together. The whispers of the enchanted isles would carry their story far and wide, a tale of bravery, friendship, and the magic that lies within the heart.

As the sun sets upon another day in Eldoria, casting a warm glow over the isles, the children gather once more to reflect on their journeys. They share tales of their triumphs and tribulations, their laughter mingling with the soft rustle of the leaves. In that sacred space, they understand that the heart of courage is not just about facing dragons or embarking on grand quests; it is about the connections forged through friendship, the lessons learned through hardship, and the unwavering belief that they can rise together, no matter the odds. With each story shared, the heartbeat of courage grows stronger, resonating throughout the enchanted isles—a powerful reminder that within every heart lies the capacity for greatness, waiting to be unleashed.

Discovering the Hidden Paths

In the heart of the Enchanted Isles, where the waves kissed the shores and the stars twinkled like scattered gems, there lay a tapestry of hidden paths waiting to be discovered. These trails, woven through ancient forests and over misty mountains, were more than mere routes; they were the lifelines of friendship, courage, and the boundless magic that pulsed through the land. Every twist and turn held secrets of the past, whispers of adventures yet to unfold, and the promise of connection for those brave enough to seek them out.

As our young adventurers, Lira, Tink, Liora and Finn, set foot on the first path, they felt an electric thrill coursing through their veins. The air shimmered with possibilities, and the foliage seemed to beckon them closer. Each step was a reminder that the world was alive, breathing with stories waiting to be told. They learned that hidden paths often required more than just physical exploration; they demanded an open heart and a willingness to embrace the unknown. This journey was not merely about reaching a destination but about discovering the resilience and strength that lay within themselves.

Their first encounter on the path was with a gentle creature named Lumina, a small, glowing fox who had lost her way. Lira, Liora and Finn quickly realized that the hidden paths were not just about their own adventures; they were also about the bonds they formed along the way. Tink helps Lumina find her home, and they not only forge a new friendship but also discover the joy of selflessness. In the enchanted world, every act of kindness echoed throughout the Isles, creating ripples of magic that would guide others on their journeys.

As they ventured deeper into the woods, the paths became increasingly intricate, revealing unexpected challenges that tested their courage. They faced daunting obstacles: a rickety bridge swaying over a chasm and a dark cave filled with echoes of their fears. Yet, with every challenge, they all learned the true meaning of bravery. They realized that courage was not the absence of fear but the determination to move forward despite it. Each step they took was a testament to their growing strength and their unwavering belief in one another.

In the end, the hidden paths of the Enchanted Isles transformed Liora and Finn into more than just adventurers; they became guardians of magic and friendship. They discovered that the real treasure lay not in the destination but in the journey itself—a journey filled with laughter, lessons, and love. As they emerged from the woods, they understood that the hidden paths would always be there, waiting for new explorers to uncover their secrets. The whispers of the Isles echoed in their hearts, reminding them that, together, they could overcome any challenge and illuminate the world with the glow of their friendship.

The Guardian of the Island

In the heart of the mythical archipelago known as the Enchanted Isles, where emerald forests kissed the azure seas, there resided a guardian unlike any other. This guardian, a majestic creature named Aeloria, was a shimmering dragon with scales that reflected the colors of the sky at dawn and dusk. With wings that spanned across the horizon, Aeloria served as the protector of the islands, watching over its inhabitants with a fierce yet gentle spirit. Legends whispered of her presence, describing how she soared through the clouds, her roar echoing like thunder, warning all who sought to disturb the harmony of this magical realm.

Aeloria's bond with the islands was forged long before the first settlers arrived. It was said that she had been born from the very essence of the land, imbued with the magic of the winds and the whispers of ancient trees. Her wisdom was unmatched, and the creatures of the isle looked to her for guidance. Whenever storms threatened to ravage the shores or dark shadows loomed over the vibrant villages, Aeloria would rise, her powerful wings dispersing the clouds and restoring peace. The people revered her not just as a protector but as a friend, often gathering to share stories of her bravery and grace under the starlit sky.

In the village of Lumnara, nestled at the edge of the enchanted forest, a group of children would often gather by the shimmering lake. Here, the trio sat among the others, their eyes filled with wonder as they awaited their guardian's arrival. They shared tales of Aeloria's adventures, dreaming of the day they would encounter her themselves. One fateful evening, as the sun dipped below the horizon, painting the sky with hues of orange and purple, the children's wish was granted. Aeloria descended gracefully, her presence illuminating the night, and at that moment, the air crackled with magic. The children felt a rush of courage as they approached their guardians, their hearts beating in synchrony with the rhythm of the island.

Aeloria, with her deep, resounding voice, welcomed them with warmth. She spoke of the importance of friendship and courage, weaving tales of bravery from ages past. She shared the story of a time when darkness threatened to engulf the isles and how the unity of its people, along with her unwavering strength, restored balance. The children listened intently, their imaginations ignited by the magic of her words. Aeloria encouraged them to embrace their own inner strength, reminding them that even the smallest act of kindness could create ripples of change across the world.

As the night deepened, Aeloria gifted the Trio children a shimmering scale, a token of their newfound bond. "This scale," she explained, "is a reminder that you, too, are guardians of this island. Protect its beauty, cherish your friendships, and never shy away from acts of courage." With that, she took to the skies once more, leaving behind a trail of sparkling light. The children returned home, their hearts swelling with inspiration, knowing that they carried a piece of their guardian with them. From that day forth, they vowed to uphold the values Aeloria had instilled in them, becoming the next generation of protectors for their beloved Enchanted Isles.

Lessons from the Ancient Trees

In the heart of the Enchanted Isles, where the sky kisses the sea, and the air is thick with magic, stand the ancient trees—majestic sentinels of time that have witnessed the rise and fall of civilizations. Their gnarled trunks twist skyward, and their sprawling branches weave a tapestry of whispers that tell tales of friendship, bravery, and the delicate balance of life. To gaze upon these trees is to peer into the very soul of the land, for they hold secrets that can inspire even the youngest hearts. Each ring in their trunk is a story, a lesson waiting to be discovered by those willing to listen.

As the children of the Isles embark on their adventures, they often find themselves seeking refuge beneath the wide canopies of these ancient guardians. Here, in the shade of their leaves, they learn that patience is a virtue, much like the slow growth of the trees themselves. These magnificent beings take decades, even centuries, to reach their full potential. The children realize that some things in life cannot be rushed; true strength and wisdom come with time, and the journey is just as important as the destination. This understanding becomes a cornerstone of their friendships, teaching them to support one another through life's ups and downs.

The trees also impart lessons of resilience. In times of storm, when fierce winds howl and rain pelts the ground, the ancient trees bend but do not break. They teach the children that life's challenges may test their spirits, yet it is in these moments that they must remain grounded. The ability to adapt and endure becomes a vital lesson, instilling a sense of courage that empowers the young adventurers to face their fears. Like the ancient trees, they learn to sway with the winds of change, emerging stronger and more united as they navigate their own quests.

Moreover, the ancient trees symbolize the importance of community. Their roots intertwine beneath the earth, supporting one another in unseen ways. This intricate network teaches the children that true strength lies in togetherness. They come to understand that friendships, much like the roots of the trees, provide nourishment and stability. In this interconnectedness, they find the magic of collaboration and teamwork, realizing that by lifting each other up, they can achieve far more than they could alone. This lesson becomes a guiding light as they face challenges, reminding them that they are never truly alone in their journeys.

Ultimately, the ancient trees stand not only as witnesses to the passing of time but as wise mentors offering invaluable life lessons. They inspire the children to cultivate patience, resilience, and community spirit as they forge their paths through the Enchanted Isles. In moments of doubt, they will remember the steadfast strength of the trees and the whispers of wisdom carried on the gentle breeze. As the sun sets behind the horizon, casting a golden glow upon their leafy crowns, the children leave with hearts full of hope, ready to embrace the adventures that await them, forever changed by the enduring lessons of the ancient trees.

Chapter 15 -The Challenge of Trust

In the heart of the Enchanted Isles, where the sun painted the sky in hues of gold, and the winds carried tales of old, trust was a fragile thread woven into the fabric of every friendship. It sparkled like the morning dew on the petals of the Lumina flowers, precious and easily shattered. In a realm where magic danced with reality, the challenge of trust became a quest in itself, beckoning the brave and the kind-hearted to embark on a journey of understanding and courage. As the gentle waves lapped against the shores, stories of betrayal and loyalty echoed through time, reminding the inhabitants that trust, once broken, could take many forms before it could be restored.

Our heroes, Tink, Lira, Liora and Finn, found themselves at the crossroads of doubt and belief. They had shared countless adventures, their bond forged in the heat of challenges faced together. Yet, in the shadow of a dark prophecy whispered by the ancient oracles, mistrust began to creep into their hearts like an unwelcome fog. Tink, gifted with the ability to commune with the spirits of the forest, felt a tug of uncertainty when Finn, with his knack for invention, proposed a daring plan. The weight of their decisions pressed heavily upon them, and the challenge of trusting one another loomed larger than the fiercest storm.

One fateful day, a mysterious fog rolled in from the sea, shrouding the island in an air of uncertainty. The ancient seer, a wise and gentle figure draped in robes woven with starlight, warned the villagers of an impending challenge that would test the hearts of those who dared to venture beyond their familiar shores. Liora and Finn, brave and curious, felt an undeniable pull to face this challenge together, knowing that their friendship would be the compass guiding them through the unknown. With a shared glance, they pledged to stand by each other, ready to confront whatever lay ahead.

As they journeyed deeper into the enchanted forest, the trees whispered secrets, and the ground sparkled with the magic of the ancients. They soon discovered a hidden glen, where a radiant crystal stood at its center, pulsating with mesmerizing light. However, the crystal guarded a powerful spell that could only be unlocked by a true act of loyalty. The test was simple yet profound: each friend had to choose between their own desires and the well-being of the other. Liora's heart raced as she contemplated her own wishes, knowing that the fate of their friendship hung in the balance.

The moment of truth arrived, and the glen fell silent. With a deep breath, Liora stepped forward, willing to sacrifice her dreams for Finn's happiness. Finn, witnessing her selflessness, realized the depth of their bond. AtAt that moment, he, too made a choice, putting Liora's aspirations above his own. The crystal responded to their unwavering loyalty, its light intensifying, illuminating the glen with a brilliance that transcended understanding. They had passed the test, not just as individuals but as a united force, stronger for having faced the challenge together.

Emerging from the glen, Liora and Finn felt transformed. They learned that true loyalty is not merely about standing by someone's side but also about recognizing and honoring their dreams. Their hearts swelled with the knowledge that no matter what trials lay ahead, their friendship would remain steadfast, a beacon of hope in the face of adversity. As they walked back toward their village, the whispers of the enchanted Isles echoed in their minds, reminding them that the greatest adventures often begin with a simple act of loyalty. Together, they were ready to face whatever came next. Their spirits intertwined like the magic of the Isles itself.

Their journey through the Enchanted Isles tested their resolve time and again. Encounters with mischievous sprites and cunning sorcerers challenged their faith in each other as external forces sought to sow discord between them. Yet, with each trial, they learned that trust was a living entity capable of growing and evolving. They discovered that even the strongest friendships could falter, but through perseverance, they could rise anew. The lessons they learned became shimmering beacons of hope, illuminating the path for others who would one day face similar trials.

Finding Strength in Unity

In the midst of a brewing storm, another diverse group of friends found themselves drawn to one another by the invisible threads of fate. Each possessed unique gifts: Elara, the gentle healer with a heart as vast as the ocean; Thorne, the fierce warrior whose spirit burned like wildfire; and Lirael, the clever trickster with a mind that danced like the wind. Initially, they saw their differences as obstacles, believing that their individual strengths should suffice. Yet, as trials began to unfold, they learned that their varied abilities, when woven together, created a tapestry of resilience that could withstand even the fiercest tempests.

As the friends embarked on their quest, they faced formidable foes and daunting challenges that tested their resolve. Tme and again, they stumbled and faltered, but it was in these moments of vulnerability that the true power of their unity shone through. When Thorne's strength waned, Elara's nurturing spirit lifted him, and when Liora's clever plans faltered, the unwavering loyalty of her companions reignited her determination. Each setback became a lesson, a reminder that even the mightiest heroes could only rise through the support of their friends, illuminating the path forward with hope and courage.

The turning point in their adventure came when an ancient dragon, once a guardian of the Isles, was driven to despair by a dark force. The friends, realizing that not only their own fates but the fate of their beloved land depended on their unity, pooled their strengths in a climactic battle. As they fought side by side, the magic of their friendship swirled around them, creating a shield of light that pushed back the shadows. In that moment, they transformed not just as individuals but as a unified force, embodying the very essence of what it meant to stand together against adversity.

In the aftermath of their victory, the friends understood that their journey was more than a quest for personal glory; it was a testament to the power of camaraderie and shared dreams. They returned to their homes, hearts full and spirits high, ready to share their stories and inspire others. The whispers of their adventures traveled far and wide, reminding all who heard them that in times of darkness, it is the strength found in unity that ignites the brightest lights. Through their tale, the Enchanted Isles became a beacon of hope—a land where friendship and courage intertwined, encouraging generations to come to cherish the bonds that empower them to face the world together.

In the tapestry of this tale, both groups of young adventurers embark on a journey that challenges them to look beyond the surface of their abilities. With each challenge they face, from treacherous forests to shimmering lagoons, they learn that the key to unlocking their powers lies not solely in their individual strengths but in the bonds, they forge with one another. Each friendship becomes a catalyst for growth, revealing that the greatest magic often emerges when we come together, sharing our fears and dreams. As they navigate through trials, the characters discover that their unique talents are amplified in unity, teaching young readers the invaluable lesson of collaboration and support.

The Enchanted Isles are steeped in lore, where ancient spells whisper through the trees and mystical creatures guard the secrets of the universe. Here, the protagonists encounter wise mentors who guide them in recognizing their innate abilities. These mentors symbolize the importance of guidance and learning, showing that wisdom often comes from those who have walked the path before us. Through their teachings, the young adventurers uncover the essence of their powers, learning to harness them not just for personal gain but for the good of their community. This journey emphasizes that true strength is not only about individual achievement but also about uplifting others and using our gifts to create a brighter world.

As the adventurers delve deeper into their quests, they confront their fears and insecurities, which often serve as the greatest barriers to unlocking their powers. Each character embodies different struggles, from the shy dreamer hesitant to share her voice to the bold warrior grappling with self-doubt. Through courage and perseverance, they learn that embracing vulnerability is a crucial step in their transformation. The narrative encourages readers to confront their own challenges, illustrating that the path to discovering one's hidden powers is often paved with obstacles that can be overcome through resilience and the support of friends.

Unleashing Hidden Powers

Ultimately, "Unleashing Hidden Powers" serves as a beacon of hope, reminding us that within each of us lies a reservoir of strength waiting to be awakened. The tale invites readers to embark on their own journeys of self-discovery, urging them to explore the depths of their hearts and the heights of their imaginations. In a world where every whisper of magic can lead to extraordinary adventures, the true power lies not in the spells or the fantastical creatures that populate the Enchanted Isles but in the courage to believe in oneself and the bonds of friendship that can transform dreams into reality. Through this enchanting narrative, the message is clear: when we embrace our hidden powers together, we can illuminate even the darkest corners of our world.

Legends spoke of a time when the Isles were divided by mistrust and fear. Villages stood isolated, their inhabitants wary of one another, convinced that strength lay only in solitude. Yet, amidst the chaos, a young girl named Elara discovered the secret of the Binding Spell. With a heart full of compassion and an unwavering belief in the goodness of others, she began to extend her hand to those around her. Each small act of kindness—a shared meal, a helping hand, a listening ear—began to weave an invisible thread of connection among the villagers. Slowly but surely, the spell took hold, and the Isles began to transform.

As the warm light of kindness spread, it illuminated the darkest corners of the realm. Neighbors who had once eyed each other with suspicion now gathered to share stories and laughter. The once-quiet streets filled with the sounds of joy and camaraderie as the Binding Spell of Kindness encouraged unity and collaboration. Elara's simple actions became the seeds of a vibrant community where differences were celebrated rather than feared. Through her journey, readers learn that true strength lies not in power or dominance but in the ability to uplift one another through empathy and understanding.

However, the tale does not end with a mere transformation. Challenges still loomed on the horizon as dark forces sought to extinguish the warm glow of kindness that had begun to flourish. With courage in her heart, Elara rallied her friends, reminding them of the spell they had collectively cast. They understood that even in the face of adversity, the Binding Spell of Kindness could be their greatest weapon. Together, they faced trials that tested their resolve, proving that friendship, forged in the fires of compassion, could conquer even the most daunting of obstacles.

In the end, the Binding Spell of Kindness and hidden powers was not just a magical force; it became a way of life for all who inhabited the Enchanted Isles. This tale teaches young readers that every act of kindness, no matter how small, contributes to a greater tapestry of love and connection. As the story unfolds, it inspires them to embrace the magic within their own hearts, reminding them that they, too, can be agents of change in their world. The Bonds of friendship, woven through kindness, create a legacy that transcends time, echoing in the hearts of generations to come.

Together We Stand

In the heart of the Enchanted Isles, where the sun kissed the emerald waters and the air hummed with the magic of ancient tales, a profound truth echoed through the land: together we stand. This principle resonated deeply among the diverse inhabitants of the Isles, from the mischievous pixies flitting about the blossoms to the wise old centaurs who roamed the forests guarding their secrets. Each creature, each being, understood that their strength lay not in isolation but in the bonds they forged with one another. This belief was the seed from which courage blossomed, inspiring even the smallest of hearts to rise against the greatest of challenges.

The story of Liora, a young girl with a heart full of dreams, embodied this spirit of unity. When dark clouds began to loom over the Isles, casting shadows of despair and fear, Liora was determined to seek help. With her trusty companion, Finn, she embarked on a journey across the magical landscape, gathering friends from every corner of the realm. As they traveled through the shimmering meadows and misty mountains, they encountered creatures that were once at odds, each with their own fears and doubts. But Liora's infectious bravery ignited a spark of hope, reminding them that together, they could shine brighter than any darkness.

As the group grew, so did their resolve. The whimsical melodies of the forest dweller sprites intertwined with the deep, resonant chants of the ancient stone golems, creating a symphony of strength that echoed across the Isles. Each member brought unique gifts to the table—whether it was the healing songs of the merfolk or the fire-spitting talents of the dragons. Together, they crafted a plan to confront the shadow that threatened their home. It was a lesson in collaboration and trust, showing that every voice mattered and that true power was found in unity.

In the face of adversity, the bonds of friendship forged by Liora and her companions proved unbreakable. They learned to listen to one another, to respect their differences, and to celebrate their strengths. As they faced trials and tribulations, their collective courage transformed fear into determination. With each challenge they overcame, they became a beacon of hope for all the creatures of the Isles, inspiring others to join their cause. They showed that when individuals come together for a common purpose, they can weave a tapestry of resilience that no darkness can unravel.

"Together we stand" became more than just a saying; it became the heart of their adventure. The enchanted Isles, once filled with whispers of doubt, now resonated with the echoes of laughter and solidarity. They discovered that every journey is enriched by the companionship of others and that the greatest magic lies not in spells or potions but in the love and support shared among friends. This tale of courage and friendship serves as a reminder for all young dreamers: when united, we are capable of overcoming any obstacle, lighting the way for a brighter tomorrow.

This story still has more to be written. Still, more adventures and hidden quests lay ahead.

A Tale of Escape

A group of Earthlings, including a young woman named Elara, is abducted by an invisible alien ship to become part of a cosmic exhibition. Facing the reality of being observed by an alien audience, they form a bond and ignite a longing for freedom. Together, they plot their escape, daring to dream of returning to their lives on Earth. As they navigate their captivity and fight for autonomy, they are tested but remain unbroken, driven by the hope of weaving their experiences back into humanity's story.

Whispers in the Sand

Amidst the whispers of the sand and the caress of the Autumn sea, a tale of survival unfolds on the shores of a forsaken island. Here, young Selene and her father carve out an existence, relying on the embrace of nature and each other. Their bond, once threatened by tragedy, burgeons under the trials they face in this barren refuge. But when the island yields an unexpected reunion, the fabric of their family is woven together once more, painting a poignant portrait of hope and resilience. In the cool embrace of a late afternoon's breeze, Selene's heart finds solace, and together, they etch a new beginning upon their souls— an indelible whisper in the fabric of time.

TYLORIN

In the oppressive kingdom of Eldaf, where elves endure human cruelty, a desperate elf mother and her child find an unexpected ally in a compassionate human. Together, they embark on a perilous escape through secret paths and natural sanctuaries, aided by the whispers of the forest's denizens. Their journey leads them to an abandoned, tranquil cottage, where they begin a new life of resilience and love. United by courage and kinship, their bond transcends blood, offering hope and peace amidst the shadows of their past.

ECHOES OF LAUGHTER, ECHOES OF FEAR

In an abandoned amusement park reclaimed by nature, five young explorersâ€"three girls and two boysâ€"embark on an adventure filled with mystery and spectral intrigue. Amid peeling paint and rusting rides, they delve into the park's hidden sorrows, blending nostalgia with a sense of foreboding. As they confront both the park's secrets and their own fears, their journey becomes a test of courage, friendship, and the human spirit. In this eerie yet captivating odyssey, the line between joy and darkness blurs, leaving them to discover whether their bonds can light the way through the park's enigmatic shadows.

SEA OF SHADOWS

Stranded on a solitary island, young Helene navigates a journey of survival and self-discovery, guided by the wisdom of her late father and

the lessons of the untamed wilderness. Amid the island's deceptive tranquility, she transforms grief into resilience, building a sanctuary from remnants of the past and forging a future shaped by love and fortitude. Through hardship, Helene finds strength in enduring connections, her father's presence ever a guiding light. Her odyssey is one of emotional catharsis and renewal, where each dawn heralds the triumph of hope and the radiance of new beginnings.